THE NATTY P. BOOKS

ISBN NUMBER: 978-0-9957345-2-4

The Dandelion Dog

For everyone who has ever made a Dandelion wish.

The little girl slept very well that night
and when she awoke she hardly spoke,
as sitting there in her rocking chair
was a sight that was bespoke.

She could hardly believe her eyes
'Wow, what a wonderful surprise!' she cried,
'but who are you and what are you here to do?'
asked the little girl making such a hullabaloo.

'Well hello there,' said the creature, 'it's very nice to meet you, do you not recall? You beckoned me back in the fall, when you blew on the flower, it gave you the power to summons me upon your call.'

The little girl sat and thought for a while about the flower back in the fall.
'Oh yes I do recall,' she said, 'One big puff! It didn't take long and the flower was gone
and as I sat upon the log I made my wish for a dog!'

'Well can't you see, that is me!' said the creature with a voice filled with glee.
'When you made your wish on the log, you made me your Dandelion dog!
I have the face of a lion,' he said letting out a great big roar,

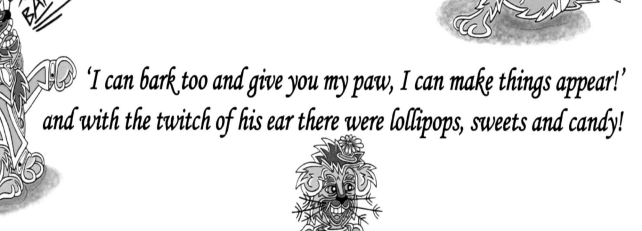

'I can bark too and give you my paw, I can make things appear!'
and with the twitch of his ear there were lollipops, sweets and candy!

'But most of all I am super dandy!' said the Dandelion dog walking on the tip of his toe and with the flick of his fancy dicky bow.

He held out his paw to the little girl who was sat on the floor staring at him in awe.
'Come on little girl, you must give it a whirl and show me your very best twirl!

then we can dance all night and work up an appetite to eat all the lollipops, sweets
and candy, but most of all you will see how much fun it is to be super dandy!'

The little girl took the Dandelion dog's paw and jumped up off the floor
and in a heartbeat she was on her feet
then took off in a swirl doing her very best twirl.

The Dandelion dog was impressed and made a heart shaped wisp pop out from his chest.

They twirled and they twirled,
they danced and they whirled,
until they collapsed on the floor
when they couldn't dance anymore.

And the Dandelion dog
let out a great big roar,
while the little girl
laughed until her
tummy was sore.

'Well little girl, what are your favourite things to do? It's entirely up to you!
But you must choose well, pray do tell, what's it to be?'
asked the Dandelion dog, waiting to see.

'I would love to go for a bicycle ride!' said the little girl, 'we could go far and wide,
through the countryside and find a nice place to stop
and have a picnic and some soda pop.'

'Well my dear, what a fabulous idea!' said the Dandelion dog.
And with the twitch of his ear a Tandem bicycle did appear.
'A seat for you and one for me too, hop on! and without further ado,
we can start our bicycle ride through the countryside.'

The Dandelion dog and the little girl sped off on their Tandem bike.
Looking rather swell as they rang their bell.
Shouting, 'Tally-ho!' as they rode through the meadow.

They looked up at the sky, bright and blue as the sun shone through.
It was the perfect day for a bicycle ride through the countryside

They rode up and down hills steep and long, all the time singing their favourite song.
They rode through winding country lanes and fields with high canes.

They felt the wind in their hair and listened to the tweeting of the birds in the air
and took in the beauty which was everywhere.

'Look over there,' said the Dandelion dog,
'what a perfect place to plot!' so they came to a stop
underneath a magnificent willow tree,
where they would have their afternoon tea
and of course be super dandy.

The little girl laid the blanket on the grass and opened the picnic basket clasp.
She unpacked sandwiches, cup cakes and French fancies.
They ate until they were full to the top
and washed it all down with some soda pop.

They went over to the lake and fed the ducks with their left over crusts.
They played hopscotch in the sun and had lots of fun.
'Wow, what a wonderful day!' said the Dandelion dog, 'but we must be on our way.'

They made their way home on their Tandem bicycle, merrily riding along,
when out of nowhere they had a terrible scare! when they were thrown through the air
after colliding with a grizzly bear.

They let out a great big bellow! then were saved when they landed in the meadow, in a bed full of yellow.

'Well thank you my marvellous fellows!' said the Dandelion dog to the bed full of yellow.

Which turned out to be, a sea of Dandelion flowers so wild and free.
Who saved the adventurous pair when they were thrown through the air,
breaking their fall on the flower so beautiful.
Lucky to escape without so much as a scrape.

'Soon these flowers will go to seed,' said the Dandelion dog, 'and there will indeed,
be lots of girls and boys just like you, who will make a wish,
in the hope it will come true.'

The little girl was amazed
and in quite a daze.
They sat there for a while
taking it all in,
thinking how lucky
they had been.

'Thank you kind flower,' said the little girl, 'you really are rather swell!
and I will never forget what you have done for us, saving our lives so precious!'

The Dandelion dog helped the little girl up with his cane
and when they couldn't fix their Tandem bicycle chain,

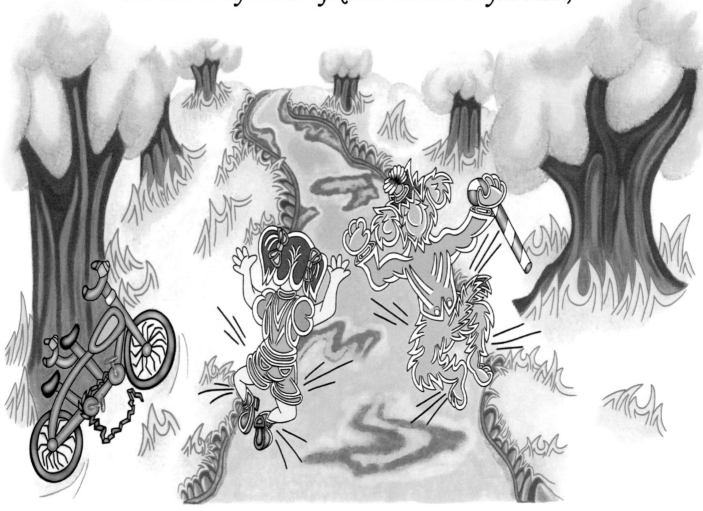

they skipped the rest of the way home, singing their song in that familiar tone.
And with the clip clop of the heel on their shoe, they even did a bell kick or two.

'There is only one thing left for us to do,' said the Dandelion dog,
'I don't know about you? but my tummy is talking to me,
so it must have been meant to be
and how very handy that we saved all the lollipops, sweets and candy!'

They both tucked in until they were full to the brim.
And to finish their perfect day they drank tea in the old fashioned way,
with an out stretched little pinkie, sipping their tea from a china cup so dinky,
being fantastically super dandy.

'This has been my most favourite day!' said the little girl,
'which I will never let fade away!

I have had a ball, but most of all, it has been so very cool
being the dandiest of them all!'

'It's time for me to go,' said the Dandelion dog, 'although I have enjoyed it so,
little girl you know what you must do, just one big puff
and you never know, wishes really can come true!'

The little girl blew as hard as she could.
And with the twitch of his ear the Dandelion dog started to disappear.
He blew her a kiss which flew through the air and landed on the tear she had shed.
Then her mum and dad came in and said, 'It's time for bed!'

The little girl slept very well that night
and when she awoke she hardly spoke,
as sitting there in her rocking chair
was a sight that was bespoke.

'Mummy and Daddy!' she screamed. 'You have answered all of my dreams!
the Dandelion flower has come through and my wish really has come true!

My very own puppy, with his fur so soft and sandy,' said the little girl,
'I shall name him Dandy!'

Milton Keynes UK
Ingram Content Group UK Ltd.
UKRC031417070424
440728UK00006B/54